How Chocolate Is Made

Written by Claire Llewellyn

Contents

Cacao Trees

Chocolate is made from cocoa beans. The beans grow in **pods** on cacao trees.

Cocoa beans look like this.

The trees grow where it is hot and wet.

Farmers grow cacao trees on their **plantations.**

3

Cacao Pods

Flowers grow on the cacao trees.
After three weeks, the flowers
turn into little green pods.

Cacao
trees in
bloom

The cocoa beans grow
inside the pods.
Week by week they
grow bigger and bigger.

The young
beans in the
pods look
like this.

5

Cutting the Pods

After about six months, the cacao pods turn yellow.

This cacao pod has turned from green to yellow.

6

The farmers cut down the pods. Then they cut them open and take out the white cocoa beans.

There are about 40 beans inside a pod.

7

Drying the Beans

The farmers lay out the beans to dry in the sun.
They turn the beans over now and then.

The beans
turn brown
as they dry.

After a week, the dried beans are put into sacks.
They are sent to chocolate **factories** all over the world.

These beans will soon be turned into chocolate.

Cooking the Beans

At the chocolate factory, the cocoa beans are put into a hot oven to **roast**. This makes them smell like chocolate.

Roasted cocoa beans coming out of the oven

10

Next the **shells** of the beans are taken off so that only the insides are left.

The insides of the beans are called nibs.

11

Making Chocolate

The nibs are **mashed** into a dark paste.

> The dark paste is called cocoa mass.

12

The cocoa mass is mixed with sugar and milk to make chocolate.

The runny chocolate is poured into molds. Then it is chilled so that the chocolate becomes hard.

The chocolate is put into molds.

13

All Sorts of Chocolates

Sometimes dried fruit
and nuts are mixed with
the chocolate
to make bars of
fruit-and-nut chocolate.

14

Sometimes runny chocolate is poured over a bar of candy.

In the US, we each eat about 12 pounds of chocolate per year.

15

Glossary

factories	buildings in which machines are used to make things
mash	to crush food so that it becomes soft
plantations	large farms where one crop is grown
pods	soft shells that protect the cocoa beans
roast	to cook food in an oven
shells	the hard outer coatings on nuts

Index